IT WAS LIKE MY TRYING TO HAVE

A TENDER-HEARTED NATURE

IT WAS LIKE MY TRYING TO HAVE

A TENDER-HEARTED NATURE

A Novella and Stories

DIANE WILLIAMS

TUSCALOOSA

The University of Alabama Press
Tuscaloosa, Alabama 35487-0380
www.uapress.ua.edu

Published by FC2, an imprint of the University of Alabama
Press, with support provided by Florida State University and
the Publications Unit of the Department of English at Illinois
State University.

Address all editorial inquiries to: Fiction Collective Two, Florida
State University, c/o English Department, Tallahassee, FL
32306-1580

Cover design: Susan Carroll
Book design: Susan Carroll, Matt Mayerchak and Tim Lantz.
Typeface: Adobe Garamond

E-ISBN: 978-0-8173-8051-9 (electronic)

Cataloging-in-Publication data is available from the Library of
Congress.

ISBN: 978-1-57366-140-9 (paper)

Acknowledgment is made to the following publications in which these stories first appeared, some in different versions and sometimes under different titles.

Bard Papers, Boston Review, BOMB, Both, Bridge, The Brooklyn Rail, Conjunctions, Denver Quarterly, Encyclopedia, Vol. 1 A–E, Fence, Hunger Mountain, Land-Grant College Review, Parakeet, Shade, 3rd bed, Verse.

CONTENTS

Again, you decide what appeals to you.

—JO IPPOLITO CHRISTENSEN

ON SEXUAL STRENGTH

A Novella

THE WIFE WOULD
COME TO US

Mr. Bird was sexually strong. That sounds good. Three—four times a night—he'd wake his wife up and thereby pass himself off as a man who encourages one to get certain ideas.

The wife would come to us and cry! That sounds harsh.

They're all dead now and perhaps I am.

"She is not a slut," Bird had said, when he introduced me to his wife.

From his wife we heard she spent her life obtaining troubles.

Mrs. Bird's name was Blanche. I am the neighbor.

My eyes are brown with a dash of green, with a dash of gray.

2

"STAY FOR LUNCH!"

One late morning when Mrs. Bird came over, I said, "Stay for lunch. Why won't you stay for lunch? Do you want to stay for lunch?"

"No," she said.

I did not manage to exit the room. It may have been that I opened my trousers and I regarded my long penis.

Blanche smoothed out her blouse. Her blouse was very lavish. Lavish? I mean that her blouse was very large and very clean!

The noise of an airplane engine rubbed at our heads.

Her hair she kept off of her forehead with a headband.

My semen dropped onto Blanche's beige slacks.

3

REDDISH SKIN AND
THIS RED FLESH

Hell, I had been putting things into myself and things were coming out of me and I couldn't close enough up.

Blanche had reddish skin and this red flesh.

I was very worried about sex, because, you know, I'd never had any formal training.

I offered her a molasses nog.

She wept and scrubbed at her slacks with a dishtowel.

Blanche, who is a big-busted woman, neatened herself. I do not know why, but in my big kitchen back then, almost from the start of her visit, I was thirsty for embarrassing moments.

We sat in the room and I tried to attract her. It's fully air-conditioned for summer.

She wiped her cheek with a blue sponge from the sink. Her short pigtail was tied with a red ribbon hanging down her back.

OH, IF YOU WANT, YES

I live in the domicile I did back then and at the upper end of my property is Voight Street.

I've still got the damask curtains and the mahogany cabinet, the flowering currants and winged euonymus, the inkweed, and my downy serviceberry.

I am an American fur sales manager.

My mishap with Blanche Bird could have been shrugged off. Oh, if you want, yes, I did shrug it off.

At any rate, Blanche even returned and she said she appreciated many of the things I had done for her.

My wife was sick and she stayed in her room.

I brought out my silver sedan and asked Blanche to take a ride. After questioning her, it appeared we'd go.

The state trooper found us and returned us to my home.

5

BOTH WERE BUSY WITH THEIR PENISES

I heard myself called by name. My wife was in the vestibule acting uplifted by daily wear and tear.

The pets we own, I noticed then—one with a tan muzzle, the other with a dark brown muzzle—both were busy with their penises.

"Do you want to be petted?" I said. "Then come here." They have pointed small snouts and erect ears.

Neither of—neither, none of us, we did not, nor did the Birds have children.

They're like little snails without their shields.

I KNEW I LIKED SEX

I went outside to toss the slugs off the lettuce and Blanche excused herself.

Try as I may, I was going over my morning stuff.

I knew I liked sex. I just couldn't get enough practice.

I wouldn't be surprised if many, many people know the whys and the wherefores of the modern methods for sex—up-to-the-minute, well-balanced information.

Well, my wife has a customary sympathetic manner and she enjoys breast play. Her mother told me.

Somebody said if you bury a bottle of beer, all of the slugs will leave your lettuce alone and they will drink your beer! Now there were so many slugs it was just crazy!

7

A VERY PERSONAL
MATTER

The afternoon at the factory was quiet. Athena brought a big pie and made coffee.

I am a perfect bore. That sounds harsh.

For the hundredth time, my factory is in the rear, past the showroom.

I was happy to get home as early as I planned.

My wife was seated, maybe, with her hands at her crotch. "If my life is ruined," she said, "it was the right thing to do." She smiled over it.

This—you can see—is a very personal matter.

I am Enrique Woytus and nothing remained for me except to figure and to doodle into a space between a few hours earlier and the next moment.

At this moment my wife offered that she did not feel influential.

8

FRUITS AND FLOWERS

The Birds, on the other hand, went out a lot. And they even traveled to cities in the north and stayed at hotels.

Sight seen! At the back of the house, between clipped hedges, there are fallen fruits and flowers. Let it remain so.

In point of fact, this is a story dominated by activities going smoothly before the interruption.

To this day I think I hear a bird's wings flapping or a dog shaking his body in the showroom.

9

"DON'T YOU THINK THAT WILL BE NICER?"

Mr. and Mrs. Bird were visiting us. Mr. Bird said to me, "I think you're excrement."

I had just kissed his wife Blanche, either on, down inside, or near her collar. On my mouth, her flesh felt much to my liking. She had a tiny amount of hair dragging around her neck and one or two small, dull dinner rings on her hands.

When the Birds arrived we had opened windows, saying "Don't you think that will be nicer?"

Those were the days when the troubles were gradually beginning to fit the occasion.

Before throwing open the door, I had cooked a tropical supper, and I had been looking forward to a vacation.

Mr. Bird made a comment about the smell of mold in the house, about which I am very sensitive.

I thought to suck my pipe and I invited all of them to have a drink.

10

GUIDE MY HEART!

I pulled myself back from politeness.

"We are not your guests," Mr. Bird said.

Guide my heart! I had labored over my wife and I had labored over his wife, using my back rim circular spreading.

This is a mercy how I defended myself in the combat. I did not get really wet. It might have been only a few drops.

BOTTOM TO TOP

I got down and went to the bathroom to clean up. I changed my garments, bottom to top.

The first part of my body hit was my head—next my happiness, my thoughts, my fears. I suffered a concussion. Was knocked out for a quarter of an hour.

I ate a lot of fruit as a remedy. I had pain in the spleen.

MY WIFE SAID

The house behind you—where you see craft items and the specialty products on the lawn—is where the Birds used to have their activities and their intercourse.

The street is arched over with trees.

My wife—my wife is resigned to a life somewhere between laughter and tears. "We'd all be blamed," my wife said, "if we were never misunderstood."

To my credit, at the factory, the in-rack was filled.

13

I HAD TOSSED IT ASIDE

The morning when the Birds made another entry had brought cooling seas and high altitude winds.

I wonder the head of the penis has the most nerve endings. I had tossed it aside, moistened.

Rudy, the Birds' large pet with rough fur came in. The door to the patio was open. Mr. Bird moved the table. Sure enough, there I was, but nothing appeared more firmly rooted than did Rudy with his caramel face.

I lowered my head while my neighbors advanced.

"You go back home!" Mrs. Bird told her husband.

14

COLDLY IGNORED

A letter from Blanche arrived which highlighted what I felt had been coldly ignored.

Dear Enrique,
  Your skin was not broken, but you call your doctor!
  (The rest of the letter from Blanche was chatty.) *We are in the North and the coffee shops are better than those we have at home. Constipation is another reason the travel is not so simple. Nothing to do is another reason for the same problem, in one sense.*
                                                    Blanche

I read the letter twice. I had the letter from Blanche and I was busy all day and enthusiastic.

DEAR BLANCHE

Dear Blanche,
I am doing and planning heartfelt, helpful things for
myself.
What suits me is a moment for something to enjoy.
Enrique

I really felt ill. I wiped out the back of my throat with my finger.

16

GOOD BEHAVIOR CAN
COME ON

Dear Blanche,
    You are not fortunately at home. Listen, good behavior can come on slowly in certain types. Do you know the reason for this letter? This is a roundabout way to talk to you, to be calm and to be reassuring.
                                                    Enrique

I did not open Blanche's next letter to me at once because one of the worst days of my life was over.

BLOOD-BLACKENED
CORDS

Things get my attention and I horse around into them!

My job includes giving moral support and I also need to make an impression on the customers.

I thought I should leave on vacation.

That night, at home, my meal with my wife would begin slowly and routinely as usual.

When Mr. Bird arrived, he was off-color.

He wore blood-blackened cords and requested the whereabouts of Blanche. I said I could conclude that I had not ascertained her location.

Which of us is wise in the solemn hour?

18

A YOUNG GIRL WHO
MARRIES

The next letter from Blanche:

Dear Enrique,
Can I be honest? Truthfully, take today for instance.
I am ashamed of it. This is what I want and nothing
else, to feel like a young girl again who marries. I know
you are close to the edge and I am up North and I can-
not get your answers.
Blanche

"SILVER BACON," "SCRUB"

I was unaware the envelopes addressed to me did not interest my wife. My wife wrote, at this time, two new songs that have since become hits: "Silver Bacon" and "Scrub."

She fills our home with the sound of triumphs we must endure.

I wrote Blanche a discouraging letter that like the others she'd receive when she returned. I always imagine I am able to explain what I mean by my words.

Dear Blanche,
  I was just kidding around.

                    All yours,
                    Enrique

20

COLD CUT

After that, like a beauty, Blanche Bird passed close to my house. I followed her to the post office. She was eating what looked like a cold cut sandwich.

She didn't see me. Nobody thinks of a ghost of a chance as a real chance.

In advance of their deaths, the following communication arrived.

Woytus,
    Two o'clock, Saturday you are expected.
                                    B. Bird

21

THE Bs

The handwriting was large and cordial-like. The signature matched the script of the text except for the *B*s, which went over, round about, and hooked and pinned each other up, like they were sexually stimulated!

It seemed wrong-headed to miss an interesting event. There's an old saying: The back foot does not leave the ground until the front foot is planted.

I took Treat along on the leash. I went there posing as a threat, in a series of actions, passing small grave-fields, mainly mounds.

2 2

THE ODOR OF FAT

I tried to console myself, but I was not the one doing the praying.

"God forgive you!" Bird said. His lips were puffed and his eyebrows close by his hairline.

The weather made it possible to go indoors. It had started to rain. I followed them past the goutweed and the flame honeysuckle at their front door into the house where there was the odor of fat.

There were drop doughnuts in the kitchen on a tray, draining. There were stools, low tables, high furniture, a multi-colored woolen carpet with an allover pattern of cup-and-saucer vine.

Bird said, "My wife wants to marry you!"

Was I duty bound to her? For there is no pot so crooked that it cannot be fitted with a crooked lid.

Fret langsam und du ahnst nicht was du bepacken kannst.[1]

---

[1]Eat slowly, and you'll be surprised what you can pack in.

23

THE HOUSE RULES

Blanche went into the dining room to get a breather perhaps. The house rules were posted there. There were loop back and fan back chairs.

Although Mr. Bird looked somber, I could see he had just put food to chew into his mouth.

The Birds' rules were detailed in adult handwriting and were posted inside a frame.

The minimum I need for the zest for life consists of nothing less. I took a stick from the collection inside their front door.

24

"I'LL KILL YOU!"

"I'll kill you," Bird said. "I'll kill your dog."

It didn't feel like such a hard blow.

I was eager to get to the garage after checking for my keys and my wallet.

My dog at some distance stayed with them.

I had opened my big mouth. I had briefly explained the marital duty and falling in love in a speech—one to one and a half minutes in duration.

This is like the lure for the Japanese beetles. They fly toward it and once they are there, they fall into the bag and they don't get themselves out.

I have, in other words, I have spent the whole of my life permitted to love with plenty of variety, like a camel who whizzed along in the desert.

They were neighbors one should and one does love. There is that old saying.

25

I WAS ACTUALLY
HORRIBLY WEAKENED

I had been given a push. There were demands on my skill and on my ability in the garage. Below my knees, I was actually horribly weakened.

Why, how did I get back into the Birds' house? I ask myself, What is the source of all blessings?

Inside their house Blanche was breaking new ground. She was hard up against her value as a human being and she could not last much longer. She wore a middy and fashionable Bermuda shorts. The buttoned breast pockets of her husband's shirt were packed with things.

Mr. Bird is a civil engineer and there was a thick unclean blueprint on their kitchen chopping block. He said, "I screw back!"

26

I HAD RUN UP THEM

At every change of direction at the upper part of the stairs—I had run up them—I saw the balustrade and fine flock paper.

One wall had a pastel portrait bust of Blanche in profile. Her facial skin was pink and white and her bare chest, pale yellowish brown. To this day it remains a moot point how it was I felt so at home in their house. She had this metal in her character, you know, which made her point of view stand firm or made it altogether too unusual for her to manage.

⟨ 27 ⟩

MY HEAD, MY SPINE

My assessment of grip pressure and other factors led me to believe my head of humerus might have been broken or my spine of scapula, but I was mistaken.

28

FIFTY-TWO OR
FIFTY-THREE

Blanche is either fifty-two or fifty-three years of age when she dies. Mr. Bird was sixty years when he died instantly.

Meanwhile, Stella is dead and Rose is dead. Ruth and Hy are dead. Willie is dead. Harold is dead. Al is dead. Yale is dead. Jon is dead. Harvey is dead. And Patricia and Bob are dead recently.

"OUR POSITION IS HOPEFUL"

I keep a diary of events. In my pocket diary I just read, "Our position is hopeful."

The cliffs were probably green with plants, huge deer, trees, and fish lizards are up there.

I saw the same cliffs and lights close by. There was pressure putting me back. I was sitting in McDonald's because I needed to get off of my feet because my ankle was badly twisted. My calf was bruised. Something out there was green and left hanging alongside the paved lot. It is not clear how people disregard all of the indications of danger.

30

AFTER DOING SOME
HARMFUL THINGS

After doing some harmful things, I made a pencil mark to begin the vacation plan. Later, I added headings.

Against this backdrop, my wife and I, we took up two tiles in the hearth. Don't look at me like that! The body had been kept out of all air and light.

The dead body was not Blanche Bird.

This event took up many months of our time.

Certainly nobody may be hidden from my wife Bernadette. Even so, Bernadette nearly died of it that time. It didn't occur to her to stop trying for the name of the deceased. She couldn't speak it without brimming over because she wanted to spill the beans.

The house was so full of tramping, and splashing, pretty chintzes, and the motor sound.

31

I SAW A HAWK

Bernadette was sitting by her rock crystal sphere in front of the roll-up blind.

I saw a hawk through the window lose its footing and fly.

"Go ahead of me on the stairway," Bernadette said.

We have a half-tester bed and jugs and bowls on the side table.

A claw caught her knee and both Tammy and Treat jumped up on her and I sweated. It was like my trying to have a tender-hearted nature.

This is how love can be featured.

I ALSO SAW THE DEUTZIA!

Over the centuries people live happily and make pictures of it. I thought I might be witnessing some of this.

I saw trees I didn't recognize from the window, but I also saw the deutzia!

My trouser was stained and some of the color was on my carpus.

We are pleased to get all over this on a regular basis.

I found myself with pain, exactly like a burn, chair-bound and with a slightly twisted trunk, my thigh to the flank of my wife. Both the physical and the emotional elements almost forced me to have moderate satisfaction.

I lifted my testicles. Maybe this will put balance into the story.

THIS MAY PUT BALANCE
INTO THE STORY

A red, long-haired dog—who didn't belong to the Birds—may put balance into the story. He belonged to the other neighbors down the hill. He was—I can't get the breed. Irish setter is what he was, named Flame. He was very often around the house. These neighbors never took care of him and he loved to be around the house and my wife would feed him and then one day we had a barbecue and we prepared steaks and put the herbs on, ready to go to the grill, and, then, when the crucial time came—the steaks and Flame were gone! I suddenly flashed on Flame.

I WAS UNDRESSED AND LISTENING

I was undressed and listening to soft music. My wife was pleasant and smiling. She has pin veins in her legs that I especially like. My reason for loving her has been brought under control.

I did some upward pulling with the pulp of my fingertip beneath the opening at the end and dampened myself.

With a rug over her knees, she had held out her arms to me. But you ask yourself: Where does one end begin and the other end end?

DAT IS SCHENE

I have swollen finger and toenails, dry mouth. *Einer allene, dat is nich schene. Aber einer und eine und dann allene, dat is schene.*[2]

I had lost the feelings of being swept and/or of being pushed—which I often look forward to for more of. There was a cold front and the seeping around of moisture and lowland rain. It was sort of a night. Bernadette used her clear stone for gazing.

An interesting point about crystal-gazing is that the image usually is not where you'd expect it to be—inside of your head! It is inside of the ball. Our ball could show us any of our experiences.

We could see ourselves in the short dry yellow grass in our own yard. And we saw a cougar, a barn owl with yellow eyes, an ape. We were stared at by an ape. Two unknown persons came through the yard, too. One was lightly crying, the other one was alarmed, I think.

---

[2]One man alone, that is not pleasing. But one man and one woman and then alone, that is pleasing.

A SIGN THAT SAYS
WELCOME

I was staking out the area. I was figuring how they were in relation to the sun. When I saw them I said, "I'll never get them out of here." I think it took me two days. But the feeling after—I am extremely proud of myself.

STORIES

THE GLAM BIRD

That's the way to eat lunch. We shared the macaroni and cheese. We both had the pestilential drink. The forest beyond is green. The table is brown. There is more than one coyote, it's a dog.

We walked barefoot on the pebbles. We looked at the bleeding hearts. My mother cooks bacon. My father makes foreign foods, pies, preserves, croquettes, and all the equivalents.

A car pulled into our driveway and the tires' contact with the pebbles sounds like lucky me counting out my paper money.

I think I'm modern. I've got to where I am today by going around being pretty. Aren't the houses nearby like blankets of glittering buttons? The sky is like a nose that's been pierced as a mark of prestige. I am like a woman who wears a hat medallion!

Three of us deeply believe in me.

WHAT A GREAT MAN LEARNED ABOUT REFLECTION AND EMOTION

There is a little money for him and a deficiency of sex.

A tad unwisely he supervises his little infant and he fumbles with its little foot.

Now let us suppose, no matter how right, he has a mush of understanding which is a false alarm because on their way to him are a little more wealth and a little health.

SWEET

It was so sweet of you to come. I am glad you are here because otherwise I'd be so lonely.

To get me here they had to pick me up off of the sidewalk and put me into the limousine and I tried to stop them from doing that.

One assumes there is an end to this initial phase.

I saw Lesley and asked to talk to her because she is usually nice. She just wants to be finished with this and to become a doctor. For some time now she's been considering that employment.

The man remember I told you about?—who calls me?—called me and he wanted to come over and I told him that now really wasn't a good time for me to have sexual relations, but he came over and what we did was peculiar, not very good, very odd, not right.

He said, "I always tell them hot! hot! hot! Otherwise it's cold. What is the matter with you?"

(I can't believe I told you that.)

There is in his face a dingy hopefulness. As the afternoon increases itself, of course, he is hopeful.

At Bloomingdale's, he put tinsel down the neck of my jacket in the back so that he wouldn't lose me.

He is tall. He has red hair and a goatee. That's what he looks like. I met with him this morning and at length we discussed that things have not been going swimmingly.

He is standing right here. In level flight he is faster. He is probably flying out of here on Friday. He's a pilot.

I have more of the story of my life and not much of his. He barely does a thing, and then he goes ahead and does it.

He is plenty sore when weather keeps him from traveling with the wind. He hit the ground to avoid hitting another biplane. He burnt his hands. He had a fracture of the skull—I mean scalp wounds—and then what adds to the confusion is the dreamlike crack that developed on his head which some call a gash, others say it is the invisible damage.

I think it will be hard to give you an accurate report—a gross report, yes.

I sleep for a few hours, turn around and drive all the way to Baltimore without stopping and run into Chester. We are sitting at a front table and I feel comfortable that my attention is on incredibly important matters. Equally important to me is my deepening and developing interest in national and global politics.

This is the next day and I go buy expensive silk

pajamas and two very heavy books.

Even though I'm broke I take several people with me to a restaurant. Across the street at the bank I take three hundred dollars from my account.

I get into bed when I become displeased. My brother and his wife stop by and I tell them we will eat a late dinner. I have had a bad case of food poisoning. All in all it is a fine Christmas. It's efficient and polite. Although, in the same manner a bowel movement is held back—a feeling dawns in me—which is not hiding, and which seems quite separate from my other feelings: I feel good that circumstances are well in hand, that I have returned from being alive.

THE RING STUCK ON

I drank a warm soup solution after. I felt mental symptoms. I threw up. After all, many who have dined with me have done so.

Significantly, I have a picture perfect headache and hard stool in the rectum.

Into the telephone I said, "What did I tell you?" I said, "Leave me alone!"

I ignored the bedclothes or I just endured them.

I wanted to hear his voice again. I telephoned him, but said nothing, and the spirits of the dead must have hit the roof.

A moth toiled in the pointy peaks of flowers in the tureen before I killed the moth.

I felt strengthless the next day, although I kept speaking to you!—much of it to my mind too thoroughly personal.

Perhaps it is only in a story that a woman or a

man can be amusingly betrayed.

Paving a way to the entrance of this house of brick and of stone, there are woodland trails. The exterior decoration of the house (I did not build it) is in a grayish, brownish stone and there are many ways to overstep the influence of this torsade band, awkwardly.

At breakfast, "Eat," I told myself. "Talk." I served myself salt mackerel and a little stalk with the leaf still attached to it, which I had paid for with hard cash.

The end of the line is massive. There is laurel all over the garden, as well as my dog Cyril, and the fowl who walk without the benefit of their arms and hands to swing. And, there is a live oak—squarish, nude, and badly executed—carved from one solid piece of pearwood.

I WAS VERY HUNGRY!

How often do trees move with such quick light steps? In fact, the place is pierced through with pear trees that approach the house. The efforts of Elizabeth Hodson have produced a young orchard.

I don't think you'll like it, but I like gaudy things.

The fruits of the climate and of the surface surround us and it is all very gaudy.

I have to get back inside of this house by 7:30 at the latest for human relations. I do not have time enough for my endeavors with the Hodson woman. She has a sad face now—at the *mise-en-scène*—that signals much pleasure, good fortune, and longevity for me.

And, this is the type of flesh I just ate—I ate a steak and I drank a big glass of wine. Elizabeth ate a double-bone. Then again, she takes so many pills for kidney.

She wore her black sweater with the black buttons

that buttons tightly and she wore a red flannel jacket with the rare green velvet collar.

Hot water was prepared for tea and Dark Pfeffernusse were served.

Looking up the cantilevered staircase, with its dopey newel animals, I think, Aren't some animals so cute!

Upstairs, I straddle Hodson and keep her lying down and warm. Then I get her into a warm bath and encourage her to try to void. I get her out of the tub and put a hot water bottle on the pain area.

In this position I reach over her and bring my top arm over her shoulder and then place my hand over her breast head. My other hand grasps for her hip. I hunch and I hunch and I hunch. It is hard to lie here and struggle with something I had thought was finished.

There's such a thing as recalling some of our confidential fretting or exultation. I've required myself to preserve some of that in a greater number.

A DRAMATIC CLASSIC
LEAP

Most of my romances are like this, so that I must conclude my behavior produces the poor result.

I present my problem to nearly everyone I know well and there is no solution to my problem. They ask me, "How did that happen?" or they say, "This is not right." They want to talk to me about sex, what I should know about fortune telling, how to think logically, how to improve my conversation.

I took to fluffing my speech with the details of the day, with some unrelated subjects about my health, my salary, with absolutely worthwhile questions on poetry and art.

I learnt that being partially helpful and light feels as if I am a dear, and, that whatever else I do I expel this.

A THOUSAND GROANS

To get back to my success, I am easily upset. They think I am afraid of this kind of thing.

This shows especially in a few details. Later I give assurances or I am not brooding.

I see a roundabout young man with relatively wide, entire segments and I embrace him. He is brisk and undecided. He embraces me. But I have the discovery of my success in the morning. To get back to my success, I am frantic and romantic.

To get back to my success I warn the man when he unties—I warn the man when he makes the soup because he has not slept well. He does the work of four men. He permits happiness to raise him up and to revive him and he thinks he is the greatest enjoyer of all time. His desire to eat peelings and his desire to boil peelings and new vegetables—it is an act!—it is an action!—it is a seizure!

I HOPE YOU WILL BE
MORE TIP-TOP

Soon after we can have this feeling. Thanks so much
for joining us. The room is a short, humid room. We
have not told anybody not to go in. As far as exactly
what happened when this broke out, I can tell you
everything. This evening the room smells like high
heaven, but this is not as coast-to-coast as it might
be. At this point what I'd like to do is tell you who's
here. Two men are in the room. Unfortunately, as I've
said over the years we can spend a lot of time playing
cards and yet everybody enjoys that. We want people
to come forth and to show their colors particularly.
Don't be worried about me. I am worried about you.
You're the one who's really in trouble. You need help.
I can help you on all problems of life. Why don't you
get my help? One visit solves your big problem. Don't
be worried about me. I am worried about you. You're
the one who's hospitable.

WELL, WELL, WELL, WELL, WELL

She took the bellows from me and she told me if they didn't work, she had bought them to have a practical function, but they didn't have one.

She said she wants to be around someone who isn't unhappy and gnashing his teeth.

"I am too late," I said. And she said she liked the way I remembered details of her life—the other end of the expanse she'd lost track of.

I trusted her rectally, but she did not trust me.

This was clearly December. I had some sense of being excluded, given that everything around me was not mine. She inquired if I liked cheese.

Some time in January the meeting between us went well. She said she never discussed true or untrue sex with men, yet she consented. She said the charms of sensation depended upon so many things going well and the stakes were too high, that she is sexually unfit. I talk the way I walk, eager as I am to make sexual advances with my friends. I do not mean to suggest social life. (Another ineffective stimulant.)

She said, "You can call my friend S., but she doesn't speak English or you can call my friend A., but she isn't nice."

Let me tell you about our organization. We have our mishaps. It's a large team, but a necessary team—families and individuals.

I came out into the street and searched for my connection to the easy future. I mean to suggest that anything else will ever happen, will introduce fresh air, will rise to the surface. She followed me in near racing condition. She caught up to me. An effervescent cab came by.

Another sort of exquisite situation was drawing a crowd out and among the theories in town while we were busy.

EVERYBODY'S SYRUP

"She's even prettier than you are," the host says.

"You really like this one?" Mr. German says.

"Have an Anjou pear," says the host. "Yes, I do."

"You didn't like Marie?" Mr. German says.

"Nope."

"Remember," Mr. German says, "you said she will slip onto your plate like syrup?"

"Like syrup. Now the question before the house . . ." the host always says.

"What are you doing?" says Mr. German.

"I'm trying to get the food out of my teeth with my tongue and I can't."

From the storyteller an endnote: That's a Butter Nuttie in the host's mouth and his Irish water spaniel is licking grains from a pan, and, finally, squared cooled build-ings, in the square, fresh and moist, intrigue townsfolk. Serves 1.

THE EASIEST WAY
OF HAVING

They are not like you.

This is what occurs. Fancy-work.

Under no circumstances is sexual contact permissible.

They use smooth knitted bath towels at home, smooth knitted hand towels, washcloths. They move their bowels twice daily if they can. The husband eats very slowly. Although, I thought last night he did very well with the sandwich!

These two work alongside one another the way the pharmacist and his wife do—day in and day out—and the way Stella and Harvey did, day in and day out. It is judicious to defer intercourse with persistence.

From a card table on the sidewalk they sell necklaces, earrings, brooches for the throat, or for near the face, for on the chest—bracelets and sometimes a bibelot. Everybody's got about eight. They are all wrapped up in tissue paper, although everybody didn't figure on being so tired out, so hungry, and so sad, and so lonely.

You see the wife has permitted a sensible and complete entrance of air into the vagina.

She has a large bosom and otherwise is a small, narrow person.

This is what shall occur—a complete new set of prohibitions—because there is pretty much wrong with practically everything that they have ever put onto their table for their enemies, come to think of it.

THE LIFE OF ANY COOK

The cook verges on spooning food into a bowl as the evening flows into a glass. The cook holds out the glass.

This really thrills her. She cries, "It's the prettiest; it's the best-looking one, Mom!"

There's something else to tell and I will coordinate it.

Now in the bowl, the contents where she put them are copulative—I mean it's the finish for a raw meal—salt and vanilla, the egg yolks, and hot milk.

She baked, dressed, ate one tiny Snickers and an Almond Kiss that she had had to fish out of the trash. Made supper and now it's ten o'clock. Think she slept for an hour and a half.

A cup, a dog, a knife, a cook, a cat, a very earnest cook can get into trouble for slipping. Then there is just one more, just a moment, a sigh of relief as the light of dawn almost pours itself back into a six-cup, paper-lined ring mold.

RICE

"That doesn't matter to me if you do not trust me," she said. "That doesn't matter. Is that okay with you?"

"Of course you know now that I will never trust anything you say ever again about anything," he said.

Her voice got baby-small, so faint that it was no longer the most beautiful sample in existence. He could not have heard her. She had to have a baby, she said. Had to.

He put his open hand on her breast. His parents had been childhood sweethearts.

The woman had the chops arranged neatly in the pan and there's a small television set on the counter. She had been cooking long slender grains of roughleg when he arrived, so he hadn't smelt the perfume of the paper whites in the clay pot on the sill of the window which was a lookout onto the little bog and accumulated plant sphagnum.

She had put on her red skirt for his arrival and possibly a brassiere and there's definitely the motley ring of troubles and the deafening ring of troubles in the air because someone once said, "I have so appreciated serving you. I look forward to many years of giving you the highest standard of excellent service."

STRONGER THAN A MAN, SIMPLER THAN A WOMAN

"Take it easy, Diane," Jacques said. "What do you want to fight with me for?"

I was embarrassed. It was like appearing in broad daylight. Even in those days I worried myself for nothing. Marie-Rose ate a few pieces of the corned beef with her fingers, not showing warmth or enthusiasm. She took a dish and emptied the contents into the sink. "Do you have any sour pickles?" she said.

"No," I said.

Jacques was vexed. I will describe Marie-Rose to you. She is tough. Tough getting tougher. Very tough. Hard. I'd say hard.

I had never met Marie before this. Fran had interviewed her.

Marie-Rose put her hand on her chin, then on her neck. Jacques was embarrassed by our women's breasts I think. Jacques stood to one side. His nipples were ignorantly abused.

He threw me off balance. I had to catch my fall. I braced myself against the plate of beef, which tipped. Then I saw a rib of bread, picked it up and it was in my left hand, the knife in my right. I licked my lips, scared of what might happen next.

To give a time limit, six weeks have passed since. It's not unusual to see older people get aggravated. But this happens among every age group.

Am taking this in steps—as I was telling you—Jacques (thirty-two) and Marie-Rose (thirty-six) came over in the morning and brought corned beef. I got Marie-Rose a fork and the knife. I motioned for them to sit down. Then Jacques had Marie by the wrists. Hurry up! As you mature you ought to have control of your emotions (all yummy and delicious—satisfactions). A thrill. I go through the the material balance in my rational capacity.

Oh, is it Wednesday?

Marie squeezed my arm. Her eyes blinked as if I didn't have a chance. The side of my right leg felt a kick. Her hair is long. She has a small thin bumpy face and thin lips. Hitting, kicking, hitting and pushing. She scratched me.

I noticed blood on me. My groin hurt.

Those are the quarrels with Jacques and Marie. I told you about them because you interest yourself in what happens when men form part of the goods exchanged between strangers. I mean the weird, old-timey men, under all sorts of disguises, who've not been heinously altered.

THESE BLENCHES GAVE
MY HEART

Life is fair I must confess. I am indebted to Erika Amor for the years 1946 and 1947 which were marked by the full flowering of the fairness. It can be expressed thus—that she did not imagine me a shy person, determined not to disobey. I had an idea she liked me and I chose her.

Her father said, "Stay with my daughter."

I agreed to, not impolitely. Lots of times it was a pleasure to be with her and I was frightened. (Some days they tell you what you said and that makes the blood flow out of your face so that all of the color goes out of your face.)

She accepted a glass of liquid and I took her to the window where she talked.

"Bring me the towel," I said. "You can lie down here instead of there."

Arms folded up over her torso—being thoroughly

stretched through the torso—her hips are stuck. Her hips roll finally. From the excitement I rub her under-lip. I spank the girl flat. She is near now.

The green chair under the phone?—that was hers and the dark wood chair under the window?—that was hers—untouched by the sex, the ax.

Across the way is a cozy Hungarian restaurant with its Kugelhopfs and sausages and The Roving Finger Barber Shop which has been there since 1950. Much of the shop is going to be demolished to make way for Malaysian Crafts.

I feel that my only big problem over the past year has been to trim myself with enough devils, beauti-ful women, owls, and hooded figures that will be of more interest than anything else I can make clear. Blank.

THE LESSER PASSAGE
ROOM

The voices, as if we rubbed them with our palms, reassured me. I don't formally know the place of origin for our voices.

A container for holding liquids stood on a marquetry table by the bed. The room had darkened some. The curtains were closed. My Pearl Spar collaborated and lustered.

I got up and turned off the faucet and released the water from the basin into the drain. It's all set.

The room we are in runs ultramarine underneath the main block. In the main block a girl crosses the brook. Two seated humans embrace. A child offers fruit to a woman. Many vessels sail. The laurel is obtained. I've heard all about it here.

Here as elsewhere one is refreshed.

THE FACTS ABOUT
TELLING CHARACTER

Against the wall opposite, she sat with her bread and her soup, which were both of them grained, strong flavored, and the best or better than there is. The effect was cosmopolitan.

Oh, he loves her so much. He loves her so much. He loves her. He loves her so much. He unlocks the door and pads into the back garden in his silk body.

By the time he is neither too ashamed, nor too peculiar to answer her question, she has finished her daily intercourse and she is—this much must be conceded—that she is forward moving with—I don't think I have ever seen such vigorous smirks.

Here we come to the horrible part. It is pretty horrible for Steve throughout last night and into tomorrow. It doesn't look as if he paid much attention to this book, to its advice, and to its instructions. You have got to have boots on the ground for this. I know he sleeps a lot and he eats a lot. That's probably very healthy.

I think he will pad back and have grapefruit. He is hungry. Have grapefruit. It's the size of a clock radio. Do you mean it's the size of a shoebox? You can't be certain without precision measurement.

One needs a more professional atmosphere. The information minister and the people are very much against that, so that didn't happen. Everything went smoothly as silky.

FLOWER

"He is the only one you will sleep with and you two will consult with each other about everything!" her father said. "Go live with him. He will welcome you.

I am certain. Do you want to be rich?" her father said.

"Yes," she said, "I am sure."

"Susan," said the father.

"Yes?"

He said, "To get that nipple to stand up, squeeze it."

DOODIA

By day I see the fine future—the ordinariness of festivals, the house, gulping wine.

By day I dream of a real and good dog.

This is not the unknown and neither is a pregnancy, a miscarriage, durableness.

It has been raining and the houses are up on stilts.

There are a lot of stray dogs and there is a sweet one we call Bride and we fed him and he went to the bathroom and I rushed to get some paper. "He's all dirty. Clean him!" I said.

My mother laughed and she said, "They clean themselves on the grass!" I wanted her to clean him up the way she cleans me. It would have been hopeful enough for me.

I do not know what to do. I do not know who to trust.

HANDY-DANDY

"I feel fine today, actually."

"When you grow up are you going to marry some nice girl and have children? Of course you are, and are you going to make your children eat food that's good for them? Of course you are! I know that you are! Just put on the coat and go outside."

"Even if the coat will get dirty?"

"Yeh-es."

Mom and Buzz—both of whom have gossiped this week—had been sitting down to their lunch. After what seemed a long wait, Buzz, holding his side, complained of an ache.

Mom examined with her fingers, smoothing the phenomenon away. The boy set off for some good fortune along the parched pathway which led away from the pathway. Surrounded by shrubs which had stuck their thorns into him, he had climbed into them. Couldn't I get out? he thought.

He thought, breathless with the reversal of fortune, How can I be so clever? What was it my mother said? He contemplated brambles with monoecious flowers and globose fruit of woody carpels.

To him, this midday felt like his first midday, of his not being soothingly cut.

AGGRESSIVE GLASS AND MIRRORS

"I didn't know he was famous," my husband said.

I said, "He said all he knew is that he wanted to be famous." I had praised Yves.

Later that night I glared at my husband. The time limit was a few seconds. I think when you're younger the first idea you have is that adults want to talk.

My brother Joe—I was at ease with him—arrived shortly. My chin hit something.

"Do you have something in your eye?" my brother said.

"Yes."

"Go rinse your eye."

"What's the matter?" my husband said.

"She has something in her eye. Go rinse your eye."

"I should clean it."

"Yes, you should do so."

And agitate slightly. Rinse with water and wipe

dry. If laden with dirt, apply cleaner with brush. Don't vomit. Flood with water. Continued use is approved.

Accomplished a feat. The sky turns a different shade. It looks like it usually looks for weeks now. The glass roof of the sky is tilted up. Peeping underneath, I see the world the same as this one.

TIME-CONSUMING
STRIKING COMBINATIONS

The future has not yet produced anything to be happy about.

Yes, yes, they saw the bunching up that forms chewed-up gum, an assortment of pretzels, mustachios, and puzzling sex.

They are prepared for frosted coffee rings and something terribly wrong and they have just bumped into each other which signifies their marriage.

There is lip smacking even if their infant comes up and goes down covered with hair, face, shoulders, and arms.

The man wears his fawn needlecord coat under the evening dress tailcoat and the pecan brown corded cotton jacket with button-attached sleeve extensions under the white coat and the melton woolen black overcoat when their promenade begins to flood.

Suitcases have been packed and crucial packages

and cartons are labeled sacred.

They can fly and love to shock. Rain clouds are secret, hidden, hidden, secret, secret, secret, hidden, double and pleasant-faced.

The rainy afternoon is not hot, not peaceful, and is perfumed.

Pastry is fancy rolls, sponge-type cakes, egg yolk cakes with creamy chocolate frosting served with unusual, very strong, formerly-filled sandwiches that open with a bang and leap toward a breathtaking eater.

The nourishment, flapping, crammed its heavy-scented stuff.

BOTH MY WIFE AND
I WERE VERY WELL
SATISFIED

It felt unfortunately like a bite of a good meal. He likes his wife so well. The smell of beets was not easy to shake. He put his glass on the table. He said, "Most people who come in here they're weak. They want you to drink um three or four of those a day. I had to drink ninety ounces. First, it's a ball. I will tell you how it goes. They're really good with these kids. They're real witty, every one of them. I know for a fact. Who, oh, there are so many more! There are women in the world!"

"My wife never threw away any piece of toast!"

"Mine did."

"My wife is a good scraper. She isn't a good scraper, she just scrapes a lot. I'm a good scraper."

"I know you are. That's not that bad. Oh, I could. I'm going to give credit where credit it due. I lay no claim. She said um she said if there's a conflict where we live at, she'll handle it. Giant. I mean giant."

"Yes, and fun. And dishes of nuts and dishes of chocolates and dishes of cigarettes and light real water."

SHE BEGAN

She is slow-footed and her underparts are clean. She crosses the garden and sees dust which has fallen neatly into the basin. She could want to make this crossing every day.

There is a mound in the garden three to five feet or more across. She crosses over that mound. She steps on a succulent with salverform flowers and oblong leaves. She steps on an inflorescence or on an efflorescence. She crushes a dense rosette. She spares some racemes and plantlets and not because of special circumstances.

An American couple does recognize her because she is famous for her great success on the earth and please don't add silence into this because it is making me weepy—so they extend a sincere invitation to her for her to stay with them in Philadelphia and she thanks them again for the drinks and for the conversations and for their delightful, spreading, nodding, insignificant flesh, and for the palpability of the big strides they take with their mouths somewhat open.

BABY FLOURISHES

The baby spent time on a pitiful romance. She felt herself to be in the arms—somehow gathered, forcibly invited, incapable of enjoying herself, and very much in love.

OPENING THE CLOSING
MOUTH OF THE WOMAN

A penis leans on walls inside her. Faustine—that is her name—is dedicated to the rammers after she has been loaded with their meaning. A corner of her is being slightly shaped.

THE KING EMPEROR

They say they sat on the moldy border near a Kousa dogwood, under a different low-growing tree, which is the oldest tree in the story. It has arching branches, red berries, and fine-textured, robust bark.

Both were commenting that there is always something each wishes for that comes true.

He took his neckerchief off and the gauntlets, and his soiled coat—touched it willingly on the sleeve—and fawned over the woman whose name is Beth Schwenk and I am not just blowing smoke up your ass. He said, "Oh, you have been everywhere!"

People—and I do too—present stories and stories about him just to destabilize.

He had the clamber to hump Schwenk and to enjoy what he frogged or was able to wring off as a prisoner of the love scene.

There is much impertinence in trying to make

more of this public.

He's sure got a weak spot for her, but it's getting harder all of the time at the dirty end of his stick when his chances come to pass in reality.

Just to have a name like his name must be such a pleasure. He's had two chances. Now they hear him promising.

It sounds as if he's right around the corner now in all of June, even if he had to stand in the no-hope-for-you corridor.

He knows the collections of laws.

He has relief in The House decorated by Blue China Furs and semievergreen shrubs with poorly-stemmed flowers planted in well-drained soil. The House is equipped with tiles and portraits of people who see right through me. It's heartbreaking pretend-ing to be sympathetic to him. He taught his horse to jump. Yes, he's voluptuous and kind and the eldest son of the first gentleman. Some of the most momen-tous daughters and sons come from that guy.

He is popular with the people, unplain in face, and one of the great men with his plump heart so animadverted upon.

He wasn't as great as this before this rain. He will be hardly much different after the rain.

He took the candle and the blankets and is noisy and difficult because he's the fellow who lives with Beth Schwenk and what shoots forth from him he pledges is the light in his eyes. Schwenk waits for me.

I see what this is. I've screwed my head off in the middle of my neck for the royalty.

PLEASE LET ME OUT
AGAIN OF THE SMALL
PLUGGED HOLE

Her face was as useless to her as hot stew. Her breasts were tight, unripe. She wore a that's very funny expression.

Another thing, her old clothes were tight.

In a frame on a wall was a picture of an old baby. Furthermore, a tailor measured her for tunics, for a decent striped skirt, for a sash, for underwear to cover her buttocks.

She didn't dare to say what she was getting at.

Her socks were twisted. She climbed back up towards the benefits of better function and pleasure, although she was developing a head cold.

And, the woman had trouble with her socks, but no trouble with sex she could sneeze at.

Step this way. Another thing, they were awfully tight, her tight clothes.

But, uh, her hips spread as she jumped through

where all the candles were lit, where people entered, and where there was a rose tree, at any rate.

THE PHILADELPHIA
STORY

I

For several years now I have been a girl who is not married and I like to get married while I am still charming.

We open the house and gardens regularly for my weddings, although at some point I have to get reassurance in serge clothes and with my fingernail varnish on.

For as long as I can remember I think pleasantly about the town's library. So now, how about a trip to the library?

2

Jimmy Stewart wrote a book I'm reading here that puts me in mind of a November in which the whole world has a familiar large lamp—gold—that flaunts its gleam on the nineteen hundreds. His hero looks in my direction so that I'd like to go over to him and beg him to help me. I'd give him more beers so he'd talk to me about me. He really wants to be looked at and to be questioned. He says, "I am perplexing."

On a more cheerful note, while lying in bed with Jimmy Stewart, I got very excited. He's a good friend of mine, although the next thing to be concerned about is that this is being written.

3

I should give myself the name Lord. I am haughty enough.

My father was Uncle Willie. The treasures at home with everything else elegant on display include a rare William and Mary silver-gilt traveling spoon with a detachable handle, just for me and mine; an elaborate eight-piece sterling silver tea and coffee service; my gingham ruffled skirt; the silver cigarette box. Bins are filled with eyeglass cases, shoelaces, and True-Touch vinyl gloves for the manor. The pleasures are the family atmosphere.

C. K. Dexter Haven, the man I love, he's been able to get his popularity numbers up there. I need to move on this very quickly, although I petted other men, not meant for me, nearly all day, and nearly all night long. Ruth Hussey puts up with so much from me. Ruth Hussey should not put up with so much. Nobody could know how much Ruth Hussey put up with.

In the morning, for a few minutes, I sit between the wall and my bed, on the floor, ungowned.

Let's have one last drink!

Mother Lord, I see, drinks two capfuls. I drink one capful.

I look—look, I look like a white woman and there are people among us having terrible emotions.

I describe myself on foot en route to the north parlor. I admire the plate on the wall and the dish hung above it, and the long guns.

I say, "Sex-see-ool!"

And there's the bowl of avocadoes.

"Answer me!" says George Kittredge. "Where have you been?"

This was to be our real-enough wedding day, but not now.

C. K. Dexter Haven says, "You worry yourself for nothing."

Jimmy Stewart says, "She has not lain with me."

"Come, Daughter," says Pap-pah. "Hold me. Encourage me. Be strong."

EAT THE DEEP TOO!

Some of us are very good and some aren't. You know, some did their homework and got good grades. Likely they'd get a blank stare from you.

"I have to put in the medicine," the girl said. "I have to brush my teeth."

"I told them you do everything better than I do," the other girl said.

"Who did you tell?"

"Bett!"

"Bett! Bett!"

Bett started to cross her mind. Bett hung there waiting to be helpful and then Bett groaned.

In any event, people show you there is a way to have pleasure.

CUTTING AND DRESSING

The doctor said to me, "Then you have a wonderful night."

The term *wonderful night* is used to refer to the inner sanctum that has sex feeling in it.

There is a widespread misconception about the look, feel, and texture of a doctor's waiting room. The doctor asked me did I want to give him my copay now.

For the handover, I wore toreador pants and bone leather shoes with little heels—backless and strapless. I did not bend my knees, but instead stiff-walked to my sitdown in a chair. My feet I kept up parallel to the floor and I crossed my legs at the ankles.

Back at home for a cold lunch in my house with a red-tile roof, I sat in my own chair for sitting stiffly.

People are lovely things. People must have seen that my hair was in flat-knuckled curls and really inconsiderately fixed. My walls are papered with a moiré pattern. My floor is covered by split brick pavers. I've got a tea cart set out with plastic cups, lime green drink, and a plate of dry baked products.

My tot Silvanus—with bad habits and suddenly— we had set the boy free!—pulled himself up onto our lyre back side chair. Completely frenzied, the chair fell—and, because this child has never been significantly maltreated, he was stunned by the fall and he's dead.

DANGERESQUE

Mrs. White at the Red Shop showed me the beady-eyed garment, but I can't pay for it. I'm broke! I already own a gold ring and a gold-filled wristwatch and I am very uncomfortable with these. My eyes sweep the garment and its charms.

I am tempted to say this is how love works, burying everyone in the same style.

Through a fault of my own I set off as if I'm on a horse and just point and go to the next village.

This village is where flowers are painted on the sides of my house—big red dots, big yellow balls.

At home, stuck over a clock's pretty face, is a note from my husband to whom I do not show affection. With a swallow of tap water, I take a geltab.

By this time I had not yet apologized for my actions. Last night my husband told me to get up out of the bed and to go into another room.

My husband's a kind man, a clever man, a patient man, an honest man, a hard-working man.

Many people have the notion we live in an age where more people who behave just like he does lurk.

See, I may have a childlike attitude, but a woman I once read about attempted a brand new direction with a straight face.

JEWISH FOLKTALE

Around here, I see plenty of Haddock, an overall figure with his meaning growing, with a friendly frown, flanked on each side by a dog. I wonder how his bowel movements are.

I saw Mr. Haddock at the bay perhaps picking up his spirits. It's peaceful at the bay and Haddock says he does not have an ailment. He has no eye problems and perfect ears.

You know—fluid-filled space!—a bay, the bay!

Fancy cushion clouds at the bay are the same shapes and sizes as I saw when I had an exact understanding of conditions greater than my emotions.

Mr. Haddock's laugh—yeah, it is similar, but that's not what it sounds like. I remembered what it sounds like—then when you did that—I forgot.

There are a lot of young, forgetful people taking one up these days. At least I can make my claims.

Fifteen years ago there was a cloud I saw which moved around, traveled, came by, fled into the woods, exerted a strong influence, spent more than half an hour there, was free to roam, before returning to the village, where the cloud added up to a source of pride.

TO SQUEEZE WATER

"You need to," the woman said. "People should be made to say. People should be forced to say I am not a bad person," the woman said. "Can you talk about that?"

"That's very private," the man said.

JESSAMINE, EWING, ERASTUS, AND KEANE

I mention to Happy the honor of knowing Earl. I have loved Earl for months and for months and now get relief from not loving Earl.

I try to be most agreeable about this—I tell Marquis Abraham. It could have been the Marquis, but the Marquis's hair would not bunch up like that.

"Happy! Happy!" I say.

"Eat this," Happy says, "it will help you."

A loaf with a sauce.

They fired Happy, then Megdalia was fired and Sandra, not Marvin. Percy can't help me any more.

Percy once helped me. He made a hole and took my blood. He said, "I just want to cut through the fat!" He said, "Everybody who comes in here has the same color blood!"

"Take the food with you, your underpants, and the directions," one woman who created and arranged me said.

And sad to say, I don't find that very interesting.

HER LEG

"I would do anything for my son," she said. "But how little we know of what he really wants."

Meanwhile, her arm would release me. She told me what she serves for meals.

"It's all going to all work out," my husband said. "She will love you as much as she loves me."

His mother had a way of being strong, but not nasty. It was so sensuous. She and I both are short, short-haired women without eyeglasses. My husband has big eyes and he is large and muscular. I am very shy. His mother put her arm plus her leg around me—just live with it for a while. I, myself, how gladly I do.

Before long, legend has it that when a partnership works, it is no accident. More accurately, more importantly, this illustrates this: I learn more about the arts and skills.

INSPIRING ONE

I am living in a lively way with slight sobs now and then. My face squeaked under the pressure. I came to as many conclusions as possible, which puffed out loudly along with sobs. In this I was much helped by Fred. I took a look at what looked eerie—Fred. I am excited. He appears to have just had very good news. He can be receiving it every day.

If I don't refer to anything sexual, I'll be a much more likeable person, for lack of a better idea.

I am a weak woman of thirty-two in a metropolitan area. Life might be gaily spoken of.

What Fred said: "I only hope and pray. I should so much like to help you. I hope you are keeping well. I hope you will have peace of mind. Do not bother to answer me. Of course, don't reply. Please accept my sympathy. Sorry for this intrusion. I would love to see you again some day. Please never think of answering.

I am horrified."

Some months later I was about to go on a dangerous expedition to see Tiny. I can tell you about Tiny. She gave me her stationery. She's the messiest writer of bills. She used to have crinkling paper, but this time it had Tiny Boynton written on it in big letters. And she's been together with Marcel all these years and it's a very poor relationship, but then he had an affair, of course. They must have seen one another enough to have twins. I don't how she does it. I used to chat with her. She spends all day long and she takes all the dogs on this big loop. I was wondering, not knowing what her schedule was. She walks around in jodhpurs and a riding crop and totes the dogs along, and so I was desperate and I was running after her and I introduced myself and I am at the end of the world!

THE WIDOW AND THE
HAMBURGER

I can't be expected to remember his privates—a pink head or yellow head. She wipes cream off of his face and I thought, I like his haircut now. She needs to take out whiskers. I don't see why any opportunity can't be taken to do something beautifully. I look for people to admire and she is one person.

I have on Billy's robe. The robe is filthy.

I saw his penis.

She wiped shaving cream off of his face. Those two never helped the poor because they were too poor.

Sometimes he sat near her, but tried to get away if she tried to greatly entertain him.

People say the dog lay on its back, some blood near its tail.

Their house has plain bricks painted red and a shaded porch. They set their table with a cloth and the dishes and the cups—they kept them dashing off through the empty space.

If she had worried about money all the time, she'll have much more money.

For instance, your wishes are fulfilled and the dream comes true.

It is a great pleasure to be in a fascinating group.

SATISFYING, EXCITING, SUPERB

It may even be her real name. Lucky I called out to Swanhilda. I was in the bedroom concocting rocket fuel. I had a fold-down bed and it was in the fold-up position. It had like a long shelf and the bed was tucked in underneath and the shelf was fairly high and when it ignited it was just one bright white yellow flare—the rocket fuel! I used the shelf of the bed for the laboratory. I went into the hallway where there was a full-length mirror. I looked at myself, at the little scraps of thrushbeard peeling off of my hands and my face.

We should all attempt to send rockets into space. Maybe it would be a good idea to ask someone how to do it.

There was a wooden shelf. There was a wooden shelf and there was a curtain over the bed, so that the curtain caught fire and the wood caught fire but I was able to put it out. I didn't feel this was serious.

I was the one who got blown up.

I tried it a number of times and sent off a number of rockets. I tried to improve on the fuel mixture.

I may have put too much magnesium in my mix.

Well, the whole thing was like my mother used to say.

So we attached fins at the bottom and made it heavier so it didn't tumble.

I say it too!—our mother used to tell us—"A burnt child smells bad."

But after that incident I gave up my career as a rocket builder. How far did it go in the air? I try to figure that out.

Magnesium—it is not controlled, nor is sulphur and today you can buy it. Okay, and then I'm going to blow myself up.

AFFECTION

She did so very slowly and needless to say she had to go get something in the dark room. She stepped into cold liquid. There was the crap in the dark and she hadn't reached any stream! She cried!

Like her father she had an ordinary way with walking, paying no attention to daylight or to artificial light. Sometimes she would pass on her philosophies to her son. Her husband also encouraged her. His job was mainly looking for nests and getting into mischief and he made quite a name for himself. Their house sits beside a dried up tree. All the gaiety and the color she finds in sex.

OTHER RASH

Peter pets her. He says, "I said I've been experiencing a little rash on my wrists and just under my eyebrows from exposure to epoxy resins which I have been working in to complete the sanitary project. I have to get some medicine to treat it."

She says, "Good luck."

You hear the snap—it really pulls the two halves together!

There were dark red dots—they were small—and Peter said they were a nuisance all over the place on the second floor verandah. The tree had three or four branches. They were growing and he was thinking he should get rid of them. So, he showed her this— this which—he picked up one of them—well what do they look like? They look like little, little, li—very small olives, so he dug his nail into it and he peeled off a little of the meat, little more than a skin, that's it, and the pit is big, is big, and the color is—he is tasting the meat and it was dry and sweet and a little bit leathery—an intense flavor of cherry—so Peter said they shouldn't cut the tree.

It's a very nice tree. He said they were very lucky to have this very nice tree. He had no intention of using the fruit. This is a black cherry tree, so now, so what else do you want to know about Peter's cherry tree? It grew out of a cluster.

I bet you that tree was about sixty or eighty years old. The problem is it shades his whole backyard, but then after he tasted the cherries and they were good, maybe he reconsidered. His house doesn't have a cellar and the first floor is really—the tree branches are all around you, really quite beautiful, if you need this vapor.